The Magic School Bus Rides Again

Hide-and-Seek

Adapted by
Samantha Brooke

Scholastic Inc.

Arnold

Dorothy Ann (D.A.)

Wanda

Carlos

Keesha

Ralphie

Jyoti

Tim

ISBN 978-1-338-25379-5

10 9 8 7 6 5 4 3 2 1   18 19 20 21 22
Printed in the U.S.A.   40

First printing 2018
Book design by Jessica Meltzer

Meet Ms. Frizzle!

No other science teacher is quite like her.
She takes her class on wild field trips.

They go on her Magic School Bus.
It twirls and whirls and can go *anywhere*.

Where will the bus take them next?

At school today, there is a special game of hide-and-seek.

"I know how we can win against Lisa, the seeker," says D.A. "I signed up Ralphie, Tim, and Jyoti as a team."

"Why aren't you playing, D.A.?" asks Wanda.

Suddenly, Ms. Frizzle appears. "D.A. is coming on a field trip with me!" she says.

"Wow! How did you hide like that?" asks Carlos.

"**Camouflage**," Ms. Frizzle answers. She wipes colorful paint off her body. "That's how animals hide from **predators** that want to catch them."

"While you three play the game, the rest of us will go into the field to see how animals use camouflage," says D.A. "We'll call you to share what we discover."

"To the rain forest, where some of the world's greatest hiders live!" cries Ms. Frizzle.

Ms. Frizzle and the kids get on the bus.
The bus twirls and whirls. It **transforms**
into a helicopter and zooms off to the
rain forest.

Ms. Frizzle shrinks the bus to get closer to the animals.

"Look, a howler monkey!" says Wanda. Suddenly, the monkey picks up the bus. "Ahhhh!" the kids scream.

"He thinks we're a banana!"
cries Arnold.

"And he's trying to peel us!"
yells Wanda.

"Let's make like a banana and split!"
says Ms. Frizzle.

Ms. Frizzle turns the bus green and flies it to safety. Now the monkey cannot see the bus—it's hidden on a green leaf.

"Wahoo!" everyone shouts.

"I didn't know camouflage could be so colorful," says Wanda.

D.A. calls the kids back at school.
"One way animals use camouflage
is by matching the color
of what's around
them," says D.A.
"Got it!" says
Jyoti.

Tim hides in Liz's tank. He covers himself with his coat. Now he matches the color of the sand.

Ralphie covers himself in mustard. Now he matches the color of a box.

But where will Jyoti hide?

Lisa searches the classroom. She
doesn't find Tim, Ralphie, or Jyoti.
But she does find a carnival poster.
"Ahhh, clowns creep me out!"
Lisa cries. She rips down the poster.

After Lisa leaves, the boys come
out of their hiding spots.
"Where's Jyoti?" asks Tim.
Suddenly, she appears as if by magic.
"I'm right here!" she says.

"Whoa, how did you camouflage
by the window like that?" asks Tim.
"I'm wearing Smart Cloth. I **invented** it.
It can become any color I want," says Jyoti.

In the rain forest, the kids look for a new animal to learn from.

"There's a deer!" says D.A.

"Where?" asks Keesha.

"She's camouflaged. Her white spots look like light through the trees," says Wanda.

"I see a **pattern** here!" says D.A.

D.A. calls the kids back at school.
She tells them animals can use patterns
to camouflage.

"A pattern, like squares on a checkerboard?"
asks Tim.

"Yes. Now hurry!" says D.A. "Lisa is
around the corner!"

Jyoti turns on her Smart Cloth. She disappears next to a wall, and Lisa walks right past her.

Tim hides near a tent, but the wind blows away his camouflage.

"Found you!" Lisa cries.

Ralphie uses a pattern to hide in
the playground. His camouflage is so good,
Lisa doesn't see him.

"Wahooo!" the kids cheer.

In the rain forest, the kids look for
more animals that use camouflage.

Suddenly, something falls on Arnold.
"Ahhh! Is that a stick? Or a bug?"

"It's a stick bug," says Carlos.

"It's the same color, pattern, and
shape as a stick," says D.A.

D.A. calls the kids back at school. "Animals also use shape to camouflage," she explains.

"Let's do this!" says Jyoti.

Jyoti turns on her Smart Cloth.
Now she matches the color, pattern,
and shape of the balls in the playground.
But Lisa still finds her.

"You're out!" Lisa says.

Ralphie covers himself in mud.
Now he matches the color, pattern, and
shape of a log.

Lisa doesn't find him! Can Ralphie
make it to home base?

Out on the trip, D.A. is determined to win the game.

"We need more research about camouflage," she says.

"How about we dive into the ocean?" says Ms. Frizzle. She turns the bus into a submarine.

"Shouldn't we camouflage the bus in case we meet a predator?" asks Wanda.

"There's no time!" shouts D.A.

Back at school, Lisa is still searching for Ralphie. He's the last kid in the game.

She doesn't find Ralphie, but she does find another clown poster.

"Eww, so creepy!" Lisa cries.

On the field trip, the bus gets
snapped up by a hungry barracuda!
"D.A., skipping camouflage
was not a good idea!" says Wanda.

The barracuda's sharp teeth
bite through the bus walls. Water sprays
everywhere.

"We're doomed!" cries Arnold.

Suddenly, the barracuda stops swimming when it sees a lionfish!

"My research says lionfish are dangerous predators," says D.A.

The barracuda is so scared, it drops the bus and swims away.

The kids take a closer look at the predator.

"Hey! That's no lionfish," says Carlos.

"It's an octopus pretending to be a lionfish," says Wanda.

"Ah, that must be the **mimic** octopus. It camouflages to look like something that scares its predator," says Ms. Frizzle.

"Let's tell Ralphie!" says D.A.

Now Ralphie knows just how to scare Lisa away from home base. He camouflages himself like a clown and jumps out to surprise her.

"A CLOWN!" she cries, running away. Ralphie wins the game!

The class gets back just in time
to celebrate Ralphie's win.

"Thanks, D.A.! We won because of
your idea to learn about camouflage,"
says Ralphie.

"Where's the trophy?" asks D.A.

"It's in the playground," he answers.

"But be warned," laughs Lisa.
"It's camouflaged!"

Professor Frizzle's Glossary

Hi, I'm Ms. Frizzle's sister, Professor Frizzle. I used to teach at Walkerville Elementary. Now I do scientific research with my sidekick, Goldie. I'm always on an adventure learning new things, so here are some words for you to learn, too! Wahooo!

camouflage: hiding something to look like its natural surroundings

invent: to create or design something that has never existed before

mimic: to copy the actions or appearance of a person or animal

pattern: a repeated design

predators: an animal that hunts and eats other animals

transform: to change